Reading Together

OVER IN THE MEADOW

Read it together

It's never too early to share books with children. Reading together is a wonderful way for your child to enjoy books and stories— and learn to read!

Can we read this book again?

One of the most important ways of helping your child learn to read is by reading aloud—either rereading their favorite books, or getting to know new ones.

Encourage your child to join in with the reading in every possible way. They may be able to talk about the pictures, point to the words, take over parts of the reading, or retell the story afterward.

With books they know well, children can try reading to you. Don't worry if the words aren't always the same as the words on the page.

In the meadow lived a turtle and her baby turtles . . .

Old MacDonald had some ducks, too. These can be his ducks.

If they are reading and get stuck on a word, show them how to guess what it says by:
* looking at the pictures
* looking at the letter the word begins with
* reading the rest of the sentence and coming back to it.
Always help them out if they get really stuck or tired.

"We buzz," said *the Five.* Where do they buzz?

Around their snug beehive.

Sometimes you can help children look more closely at the actual words and letters. See if they can find words they recognize, or letters from their name. Help them write some of the words they know.

Now we need an *F* for "Freddie."

We read another book with numbers in it.

Yes, that was *Ten in the Bed!*

Talk about books with them, and discuss the stories and pictures. Compare new books with ones they already know.

We hope you enjoy reading this book together.

For Gran
Margaret Craig
McDougall

Illustrations copyright © 1994 by Louise Voce
Introductory and concluding notes copyright © 1998 by CPLE/L B Southwark

Second U.S. edition in this form 1999

Library of Congress Catalog Card Number 93-21294

ISBN 0-7636-0852-1

4 6 8 10 9 7 5

Printed in Hong Kong

Candlewick Press
2067 Massachusetts Avenue
Cambridge, Massachusetts 02140

OVER IN THE MEADOW

A Traditional Counting Rhyme

Louise Voce

CANDLEWICK PRESS

Over
in the meadow
in the sand
in the sun . . .

lived an old mother turtle
and her little turtle
ONE.
"Dig," said his mother.
"I dig," said the One.
So he dug all day
in the sand in the sun.

Over in the meadow,
where the stream runs blue,
lived an old mother duck
and her little ducklings
TWO.
"Quack," said their mother.
"We quack," said the Two.
So they quacked all day
where the stream runs blue.

Over in the meadow,
in a hole in a tree,
lived an old mother owl
and her little owls
THREE.
"Who-whoo," said their mother.
"Who-whoo," said the Three.
So they who-whooed all day
in a hole in a tree.

Over in the meadow,
by the big barn door,
lived an old mother mouse
and her little mice
FOUR.
"Squeak," said their mother.
"We squeak," said the Four.
So they squeaked all day
by the big barn door.

Over in the meadow,
in a snug beehive,
lived an old mother bee
and her little bees
FIVE.
"Buzz," said their mother.
"We buzz," said the Five.
So they buzzed all day
round their snug beehive.

Over in the meadow,
in a nest built of sticks,
lived an old mother squirrel
and her little squirrels
SIX.
"Jump," said their mother.
"We jump," said the Six.
So they jumped all day
round their nest built of sticks.

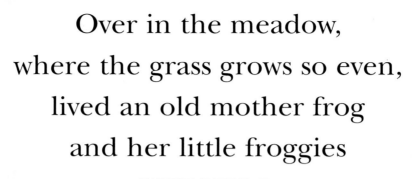

Over in the meadow,
where the grass grows so even,
lived an old mother frog
and her little froggies
SEVEN.
"Hop!" said their mother.
"We hop!" said the Seven.
So they hopped all day
where the grass grows so even.

Over in the meadow,
near the little mossy gate,
lived an old mother lizard
and her little lizards
EIGHT.
"Run," said their mother.
"We run," said the Eight.
So they ran all day
on the little mossy gate.

Over in the meadow,
by the tall green pine,
lived an old mother pig
and her little piglets
NINE.
"Oink!" said their mother.
"We oink," said the Nine.
So they oinked all day
near the tall green pine.

Over in the meadow,
in a cozy little den,
lived an old mother fox
and her little foxes
TEN.
"Play," said their mother.
"We play," said the Ten.
So they played all day
round their cozy little den.

Over in the meadow,
in the sand in the sun . . .

1  digs

2 quack

3 who-whoo

4 squeak

5  buzz

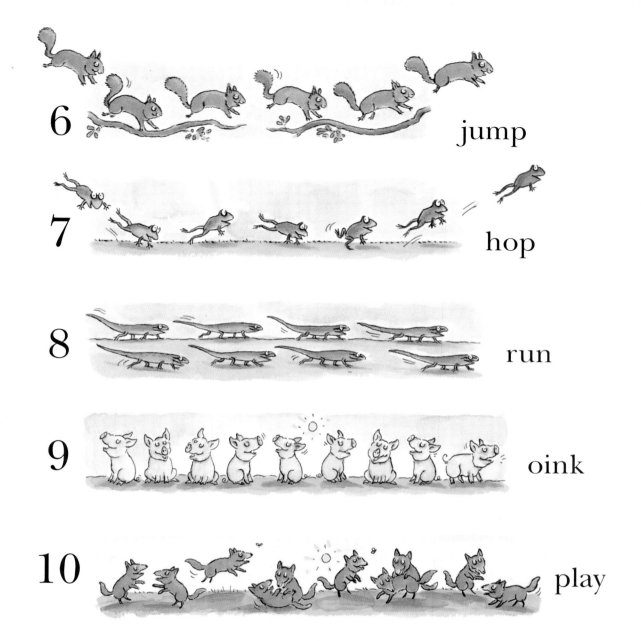

6   jump

7   hop

8   run

9   oink

10   play

over in the meadow
till the end of the day.

Read it again

Count the animals

As you read this counting rhyme, children can join in by finding the animals and counting the babies with their fingers. They could act out the rhyme, making the animal movements or sounds.

One...
two...
baby ducklings...
Quack!
Quack!

Who lives here?

You can use this picture-map of the story to match the animals to the places where they live: the barn, the beehive, a hole in a tree. . . . Children can search through the book to remind themselves where the animals live. They can also use the picture-map to retell the rhyme or make up stories about some of the characters in the book.

barn door

gate

grass

beehive

stream

How do I get home?

I'm buzzing back!

Make a counting book

Children might enjoy making their own counting book. With your help, they can draw or cut out pictures of familiar objects and put them in 1, 2, 3 or 10, 9, 8 order. You could show them different examples by reading other counting rhymes and books.

Match the numbers

Use the previous two pages to play a matching game. You can make a set of cards with the numbers and help your child match them with the pictures.

reen
ine

den

nest

hole

sand

Can you find where I live?

Reading Together

The Reading Together series is divided into four levels—starting with red, then on to yellow, blue, and finally green. The six books in each level offer children varied experiences of reading. There are stories, poems, rhymes and songs, traditional tales, and information books to choose from.

Accompanying the series is the *Reading Together Parents' Handbook,* which looks at all the different ways children learn to read and explains how *your* help can really make a difference!

     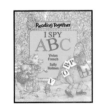